The 12 Days of Kindergarten

by Jenna Lettice • illustrated by Colleen Madden

A Random House PICTUREBACK® Book

Random House New York

Text copyright © 2017 by Jenna Lettice. Cover art and interior illustrations copyright © 2017 by Colleen Madden.
All rights reserved. Published in the United States by Random House Children's Books, a division of
Penguin Random House LLC, 1745 Broadway, New York, NY 10019. Pictureback, Random House,
and the Random House colophon are registered trademarks of Penguin Random House LLC.
randomhousekids.com
Library of Congress Control Number: 2016001653
ISBN 978-0-399-55733-0 (trade) — ISBN 978-0-399-55734-7 (ebook)
MANUFACTURED IN CHINA 10 9 8 7 6 5 4

On the **first** day of kindergarten, here's what I saw at school:

One cubby of my very own.

On the **second** day of kindergarten,
here's what I saw at school:

Two yummy snacks
and one cubby of my very own.

On the **third** day of kindergarten,
here's what I saw at school:

Three nice friends,
Two yummy snacks,
and one cubby of my very own.

On the **fourth** day of kindergarten,
here's what I saw at school:

Four chunky crayons,
Three nice friends,
Two yummy snacks,
and one cubby of my very own.

On the **fifth** day of kindergarten,
here's what I saw at school:

Five bouncy balls!
Four chunky crayons,
Three nice friends,
Two yummy snacks,
and one cubby of my very own.

On the **sixth** day of kindergarten,
here's what I saw at school:

Six teachers calling,
Five bouncy balls!
Four chunky crayons,
Three nice friends,
Two yummy snacks,
and one cubby of my very own.

On the **seventh** day of kindergarten,
here's what I saw at school:

Seven singers singing,
Six teachers calling,
Five bouncy balls!
Four chunky crayons,
Three nice friends,
Two yummy snacks,
and one cubby of my very own.

On the **eighth** day of kindergarten,
here's what I saw at school:

Eight artists painting,
Seven singers singing,
Six teachers calling,
Five bouncy balls!
Four chunky crayons,
Three nice friends,
Two yummy snacks,
and one cubby of my very own.

On the **ninth** day of kindergarten,
here's what I saw at school:

Nine builders building,
Eight artists painting,
Seven singers singing,
Six teachers calling,
Five bouncy balls!
Four chunky crayons,
Three nice friends,
Two yummy snacks,
and one cubby of my very own.

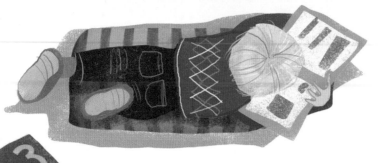

On the **tenth** day of kindergarten,
here's what I saw at school:

Ten children reading,
Nine builders building,
Eight artists painting,
Seven singers singing,
Six teachers calling,
Five bouncy balls!
Four chunky crayons,
Three nice friends,
Two yummy snacks,
and one cubby of my very own.

On the **eleventh** day of kindergarten, here's what I saw at school:

Eleven students counting,
Ten children reading,
Nine builders building,
Eight artists painting,

Seven singers singing,
Six teachers calling,
Five bouncy balls!
Four chunky crayons,
Three nice friends,
Two yummy snacks,
and one cubby of my very own.

WELCOME to
BACK-TO-SCHOOL NIGHT

On the **twelfth** day of kindergarten, here's what I saw at school:

Twelve parents smiling,
Eleven students counting,
Ten children reading,
Nine builders building,
Eight artists painting,
Seven singers singing,
Six teachers calling,
Five bouncy balls!
Four chunky crayons,
Three nice friends,
Two yummy snacks . . .

And one cubby of my very own.

Welcome to kindergarten!